ALLEY CATS

Fire! Fire!

Written by Lesley Rees
Illustrated by Terry Burton

Bright ☆ Sparks

The sun was shining in the higgledy-piggledy, messy alley.

"It's much too hot!" Hattie thought to herself, as she tried to find a nice shady spot for a snooze. Her kittens, Lenny and Lulu, were cat-napping under the apple tree and she knew from the loud snoring that Uncle Bertie and Auntie Lucy were fast asleep in their dustbins. Everyone was hiding from the sun — everyone except Cousin Archie!

Archie was lying on top of the fence,
slurping his third bottle of milk!

He didn't notice the sun's rays shining through the glass of those empty milk bottles. They were focused right onto Hattie's dustbin full of old newspapers — the perfect place for a fire to start!

Suddenly, Hattie's nose twitched.

"What's that?" she wondered. "It smells like smoke."

"It *is* smoke!" she gasped, as she saw bright red and yellow flames leaping out of her dustbin.

"F-Fire!" she cried. "Help!"

"Wake up, Bertie!" cried Hattie. "My dustbin's on fire!"

Uncle Bertie's sleepy head popped up from his dustbin.

"I must have been dreaming, Hattie!" he yawned.
"I dreamt that your bin was on fire."

"It wasn't a dream," cried Hattie. "My bin *is* on fire."

Cousin Archie fell off the fence in shock! He landed on top of poor Bertie!

"Hurry!" urged Hattie. "We must put the fire out."

All the shouting woke the twins from their dreams.

"Mummy! Mummy!" they miaowed, "What's happening?"

Hattie grabbed her kittens and put them on the top of the fence, well away from the dangerous fire.

"You'll be safe here," she told them.

Uncle Bertie knew he had to find some water quickly.

"Over there!" Hattie said, pointing to an old bucket by the fence.

"Hooray!" cried Bertie, finding the bucket half full of water. "It might just be enough to put out the fire."

"Cousin Archie!" he cried. "Come and help me!"

The two cats ran down the alley, carrying the bucket between them.

Then, with smoke billowing all around, Archie and Bertie aimed the bucket of water and let go...

SPLOSH! There was a huge sizzling sound.

"Hooray!" Bertie cried, with a sigh of relief. "We've done it!"

But suddenly, a spark from the fire landed on the rubbish next to the dustbin.

"Oh no, we haven't!" wailed Archie. "Now the rubbish is on fire!"

"Quick," Hattie said to Archie. "We need more help. Go and wake up the dogs."

At the other end of the alley, the dogs were all fast asleep.

"Help!" shrieked Archie, as he hurtled towards them. "Hattie's bin is on fire. It's spreading down the alley and we can't put it out."

But no one stirred. Archie was always playing tricks on the Alley Dogs and today it was just *too* hot to bother.

Harvey opened one eye lazily.

"That's a good one, Archie," he said. "But you'll have to try harder than that."

"It's true!" Archie shouted, desperately. "Look!"

Harvey sat up slowly.

"This had better not be one of your tricks, Archie," he growled. Then he shaded his eyes from the sun and looked up the alley.

As soon as he saw the billowing smoke, he knew the Alley Cat was telling the truth.

"Archie's right!" barked Harvey. "Quick, everyone to the rescue!"

The dogs raced up the alley towards the fire. Even little Puddles wanted to help. But Harvey scooped her up and placed her on the fence by the kittens.

"You can't do a thing, Puddles!" he said. "Just stay here."

The alley was filled with smelly black smoke. All the cats were coughing and choking. But Harvey knew just what to do.

"Quick!" he said. "Everybody to the water-barrel. Use anything you can to gather the water."

Grabbing old buckets and cans, the cats and dogs formed a long line. Auntie Lucy stood by the barrel to fill up the containers. Then, splishing and splashing, they passed the water along the line to Harvey, who threw it over the fire.

Suddenly, Lucy gave a cry. "The water's run out!"

"Oh, no!" said Archie. "We'll never put the fire out now."

The Alley Cats and Dogs stared in dismay. What could they do?
They must have more water.

"Oh, no! We're going to lose our lovely home," wailed Hattie, bursting into tears.

Suddenly, Lenny had an idea.

"I know what to do," he coughed. Grabbing his sister and Puddles, he pulled them over the fence.

"I've just remembered what's in this garden," said Lenny, disappearing into the long grass.

When he came back, he was pulling a hose.

"Mummy!" cried Lenny. "Look what we've got."

Hattie peered through the smoke and gasped. Harvey grabbed the nozzle, as Bertie leapt over the fence and raced to turn the tap on.

With a mighty spurt, the water sploshed out, drenching the blazing boxes and soaking the smouldering bins. Everyone cheered! Some of the water splashed over the cats and dogs—but they didn't care. The fizzling, sizzling fire was out!

"You little ones deserve a treat for saving our alley!" barked Harvey. "Puppy snacks for you, Puddles, and kitty nibbles for the twins."

"Three cheers for Lenny, Lulu and Puddles!" cried Archie.

"Hip-hip-hooray!"

This is a Bright Sparks Book
First published in 2001
BRIGHT SPARKS, Queen Street House, 4 Queen Street, Bath BA1 1HE, UK

Copyright © PARRAGON 2001

Created and produced by THE COMPLETE WORKS,
St. Mary's Road, Royal Leamington Spa, Warwickshire CV31 1JP, UK

Printed in China

ISBN 1-84250-197-6

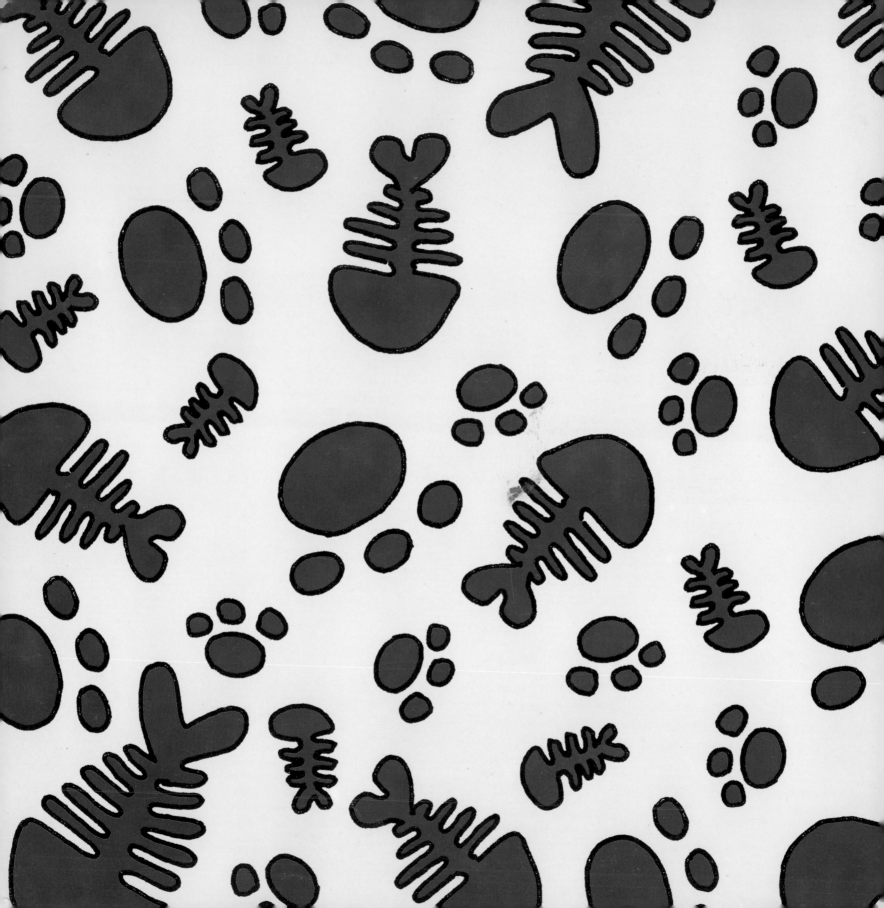